# SHARING THE ALPHA

## Steamy MMF+ Ménage

Michael Levi

ISBN: 9798826806678
Imprint: Independently published

2nd edition

Cover design by: Michael Levi

# CONTENTS

# CHAPTER 1

"This is going to rock!" Diego, a Chilean friend of mine, said from the passenger seat beside me. It was his first time going to an event outside of the city. He looked at the map once again and stared for a couple of seconds at a spot on the lower left side.

"Only about one thousand people live there?" He asked with an inquisitive face. I looked at his map, then at him before answering, "Yes, Diego. It's a small town, after all."

"I can't wait to go to that Halloween festival. Everyone at college talked a lot about it. I've got so much hype for it that I can barely control myself right now!"

I was as excited to be there as well, but since it was my nth time after many, I wasn't as jubilant as he was. "Yeah. I can't wait to meet the gals there too."

"Sucks that I won't be able to drink anything there because I'm not twenty-one yet. At least you can buy some drinks for me, right?"

"*Right?* And I guess I can go to jail by helping you out, too."

Diego shook his arms about in protest. "But, nobody has to know anything about it!"

I looked at him with narrowed eyes. "Right. It only takes one good cop to put me in jail."

"Oh! C'mon!"

"Stop it, Diego. Just enjoy your time there. The alcohol won't matter much when the girls are all over you. People there love meeting foreigners."

Diego folded his arms and sighed. "Fine, guess it'll have to do."

The boulevard in front of us was full of cars, and all were seemingly heading in the same direction. Then, the cars slowed down to a crawl before we took a turn to the right. The venue of the event was almost glowing in the distance.

As we approached it, we caught sight of a couple of police cars patrolling the area. We were clean, but I was still worried. I'd heard too often of overzealous cops stopping people from going to Halloween Forever. Diego being with us didn't help as well.

Diego didn't look as worried though, and maybe it was because he was from a completely different country.

As we approached the main gate, one of the police officers asked me to stop. I rolled down the side window and showed him my driving license. He checked it a couple of times before nodding and giving it back. Diego gave the chubby man his passport. The cop scanned the document with his eyes before giving it back.

"All good", he said. I stepped into the pedal to accelerate my sedan until we found a good parking spot. As I pulled up the car between two large SUVs, Diego reached for his backpack to stow his passport.

"What are you doing, man? They might ask for your passport even when you are there."

"Don't care. I just want to have a good time now."

I rolled my eyes. "Fine. It's your funeral if they find you without it."

Diego and I, then, left the sedan. We headed toward the entrance, where a long line was forming. Close to the gate was a dispensary with fliers and other documents which explained a bit about the area.

Diego snagged one and said, "Up here, in Halloween Forever, we have a story none of us is willing to tell. There's a large building on top of the hill that circles the area. The tale behind it is that a man once killed everyone in the building, including his relatives, before committing suicide. But, don't tell anyone about that, okay?"

"Don't tell anyone? But this thing is already here for everyone to read", he added. I rolled my eyes in disbelief.

"Diego, it's just supposed to poke some fun at the guests. Don't worry about it. Come on, let's go."

He tossed the paper back to the dispensary before we stepped toward the end of the line. Diego was a chubby short man that in no way had a chance with the ladies at the festival. I was very confident about my looks because I had trained for the whole year in the basketball team's academy.

My suspicions were put to the test when some gals walked near us. I eyed them up shamelessly, and it was enough to catch their attention. Diego did his best to look sexy with his ghost costume. I'd chosen one of a Native American because I wanted to highlight my best body features.

It seemed like it was working. I opened up a wide, mischievous smile as more gals walked across from me. Diego ran his hand aggressively through his hair when he noticed that none of the young, beautiful women were glancing at him.

I patted the poor Chilean on the back. "Come on, man. Chin up! You're gonna find what you are looking for here, I'm sure."

# CHAPTER 2

Diego already looked uninterested and tired after spending around thirty minutes in the line. I put my hand on his shoulder and said, "Look there. Don't you want to go to that house of scares? That'll cheer you up."

"Sure. Are you coming with me?"

"Me? No, of course not. I want to explore this place a bit more. Look, I've gotten your number, so if something happens, text me, okay?"

"Okay", he responded before heading to the house of scares. Considering the reputation I had heard of that place, I knew he was going to have a blast there.

I walked towards a large group of people that was parked outside a gate. As I neared it, I read a plaque that stated something about a band that was going to play here soon.

I couldn't care less about it. I had eyes only for the busty and needy women that were all over the place. Their bodies rubbed and brushed against mine, making my flaccid cock become semi-rigid.

After I walked out of the group, I looked to the side to find a cheeky woman coming my way. She was wearing a skin-tight, black dress that accentuated all of her curves. My eyes were glistening with desire.

She stopped right in front of me. Her eyes eyed me up and down. She stopped for a couple of seconds to stare at the loincloth that hid my intimate parts.

"A shy one, eh?"

I blushed, not because she was right, but because she put me in a complicated spot. "Of course not. Why would I be?"

"Seems that you are, though."

"Fine, I am. Is that the only reason why you came here?"

"Of course not. I have other reasons."

"And what would those be?" I asked while enveloping her with my right, muscular arm. She lowered her back and rested her head on my rounded pecs. Some of the people walked by staring at us.

"Want to go somewhere more… intimate?" I asked.

"Maybe…"

"Maybe!?"

"I'm waiting for someone."

"And who would that-" I tried to ask before a slender guy showed up in front of me. His blond hair looked soft and wavy against the flow of the surrounding air. He was wearing the costume of a skeleton and was a somewhat bony man.

"What do you want?" I scolded.

"He's my friend", the gal said before escaping my grasp.

"We share everything", she added.

"But… I thought it would be just the two of us", I reprimanded.

"Nope. That's not how it works for me."

I rolled my eyes. I couldn't believe I was going to have to put up with that guy while being with her. I had sex with a man only once in my life, and I didn't like it much. *Still, if that's what it takes to find my way into her wet pussy…*

"What's your name?" He asked while trying to grab my arm and then put it over his shoulders. Not wanting to piss her off, I let him do it.

"It's Lucas. What's yours, young and beautiful woman?" I asked while enveloping her against the safety of my right arm again. She let me push her toward me without protesting.

"It's Jill."

"And yours, dude?"

"It's Jamie."

"Perfect. We're now well acquainted. Wanna head out and find a good place for the three of us?"

"Of course, but before that…", Jill said while freeing herself from my arm again. She kneeled in front of me and reached with her hands to lower my loincloth. Startled, I took a step back.

"What are you doing?! We're in the middle of fucking everybody in here! Do you want the police to come and put us in jail?"

She shook her head and frowned. "Nobody will care", she argued before lowering my loincloth in the same instant. I couldn't control myself as my cock started to swell and get thicker. I looked around carefully to see if people were staring at us.

But nobody was paying attention to the woman on her knees and about to bob on my cock. Jamie was still holding tight against my arm and chuckling. I felt her hand slowly grabbing my cock. I emitted a long groan of pleasure when her tiny fingers were around my meaty member.

She slowly wrapped her lips around the glans of my cock. I closed my eyes and tilted my head back as heaps of pleasure started to build up. Gone were the worries of anybody calling the cops.

Jamie also kneeled in front of me. His hands reached for my scrotum, hanging low and looking plump. "This part is mine", he said sensually. I emitted another long moan of pleasure when he squeezed my balls lightly.

His mouth was now all over my balls. They were jumping and going from one side to the other while he played with them. Jill was bobbing up and down on me as her saliva mixed with my pre-cum. My whole cock and ballsack were now all wet.

When I was just about to reach my orgasm, both withdrew from my intimate parts. I looked down in disappointment while they picked themselves back up.

"That was just a warm-up, honey. Do you want to go to a better place? I know a place that would welcome us with open arms."

"Sure… Let's go", I said while enveloping the two of them under my arms. They rested their heads on my chest while Jill guided us. We were heading farther and farther away from all the buzz at the festival.

# CHAPTER 3

J ill and Jamie made me stop in front of an old gate. There was a padlock and a plaque that said: "No Visitors Allowed." I failed to register the warning while my eyes focused only on Jill.

She opened the gate after inviting us two to tread inside. I pondered asking why and how she had that key, and more importantly, how she knew about the place, but that thought completely disappeared when she squeezed my butt.

I enveloped Jamie and Jill in my arms another time while we headed up a steep slope toward what looked like an old mansion.

"Didn't you say this was a house?" I asked with a quizzical look. Jill looked up and responded, "Yeah and it is a house. A very beautiful and big house."

I shook my head after realizing she had just lied to me. What mattered was getting laid with her, though, even if that meant Jamie would have to play his part as well. *No matter, he can play with my balls while I pound this gal to heaven and beyond.*

I looked up and around the mansion when we reached it. The whole building looked very old, but could still stand in one piece for the next decades, I presumed. Jamie and Jill slipped out of my arms, bouncing around me.

"Guess you have this key as well?" I asked.

Jill didn't need a second invitation from me while she reached for her pocket and fished out another rusty key. It opened the large door without any sort of problems. I held it open for my two newly found friends while they stepped in.

When we reached the middle of the living room of the old mansion, the old door closed shut behind me. I looked back worried about being trapped there, but Jill grabbed my hand and forced me to go with her toward another room. It had a large bed capable of fitting the three of us comfortably on it.

Jill spread her legs open for me while she rested her back on it. I lowered my loincloth to open up space for my long and thick member. It was still wet and oozing pre-cum from the previous play we had in the middle of the festival.

Jaime abruptly showed up in front of me and cupped my balls with his hand. He started to play with them while looking with evil eyes at me. Those eyes said that he only wanted one thing from me and that he was going to get it no matter what.

I kissed his soft and hot lips for a good while before he finally withdrew and stepped aside. Jill's gaping vagina was already oozing her own, hot liquid on the bedsheets. I kneeled in front of the bed to lick her orgasm. Even without the magical touch of my tongue, the young woman was already moaning like a bitch.

Jaime took the opportunity to spread his legs on top of me. He was sitting on my shoulders and rubbing his tight, hairy asshole against my head. I tilted my head backward to give him a solid lick that made the poor man tremble in pleasure. Having lost his balance, he fell to the floor.

I looked over my shoulder to see if everything was okay with him. Noticing the young man about to get up, I resumed my action in Jill's wet pussy. I reached with my tongue to lick and provide her the best pleasure I could give. She gripped the bedsheets tightly when my tongue went inside her amazingly warm vulva.

I wasn't just playing with her, but also tormenting her. Every touch and lick of my tongue aimed at proving I was the one on top there. I had built myself to be a strong and confident man, and this moment was perfect to externalize that.

"Oh, Lucas, you're doing me so good!" She shouted while I went deeper and deeper inside her. Jaime took advantage of the situation to massage me. He kneeled behind me before roaming his hands all over my wide and muscular back.

I used my two hands to feel her soft, almost hairless legs from Jill. Her feet were of special delight to me while my fingers fumbled with them. She could almost not contain herself from spreading her legs further apart so that my hands couldn't reach them.

Jaime was now playing with my buttcheeks. His hands were probing and searching my asshole. His fingers were fumbling and fighting their way through the hairy coverage I had down there. When I looked back, I was met with his wicked eyes of sexual desire.

Having realized that Jill had enough of my tongue since I didn't want to spoil her too much, I moved up on the bed. My cock, easily longer than most men's, was standing upright and looking very much resolute. Jill widened her eyes when she saw my monstrosity standing right above the tip of her nose.

She used her hand to poke the glans before enveloping my cock between her soft lips. I emitted a long groan of pleasure when she slid down the skin for the first time. My protruding veins were pulsing with blood while her red-painted lips rubbed against the geometry of my member.

Jaime was now lying beside his friend, cupping and playing with her breasts. I couldn't simply watch him having all that part of her for himself, so I bent my back to envelop her titties with my lips as well. She fumbled and massaged my head while I devoured her milk-making melons.

Jaime's hand was also busy. It was moving up and down across the soft texture of my right buttcheek. He was giggling a bit whenever his fingers found my butthole. I had to look down at him with livid eyes since I didn't want anyone inside me.

He withdrew his hand when he realized I was dead serious. Jill grabbed my head and forced me to kiss her. My tongue and hers were dancing in our mouths. Her kiss was hot and tender, making me ooze more pre-cum all over her lean belly.

I grabbed Jaime with one arm while I lunged sideways to lay beside Jill. He was now on top of me, but he wasn't going to stay there for too long. I grabbed his slender waist and moved him to stand on top of my cock. He was as light as a feather in my strong hands.

"This is what I wanted from the start!" he shouted in delight while his tight asshole came in contact with my cockhead. I had to force him down a bit so that I was finally inside the man, but once I was there, ramming in and out of him was easy. Against the force of gravity, his rectum proved to have little resistance against the skin of my cock.

Jaime now had a wide smile across his face as his man boobs swung up and down in the air. His lack of weight also proved beneficial to make the whole process effortless.

"YES! YES! YES!" He was shouting over the loud sounds of our breaths. Jill seemed to have begun to feel a bit lonely, so she approached me to give me a long kiss of pleasure. I had to divide my attention between the two of them, but it was all the better to be able to provide pleasure for two holes simultaneously.

When I felt I was on the verge of blowing my load in the rectum of the guy, I spun my body to the left so that he would fall graciously on the bed. He looked shocked for being taken away from the action so soon, but I comforted him by slapping his lean butt a couple of times.

Jill pushed my body so that I was laying with my back on the bed again. She climbed my still rock-hard manhood to ride me as well. I began to pump her up and down as her big breasts bounced.

I now had my hands placed against the lower side of her asscheeks. I would squeeze them before pushing her upward with my waist. She was riding me like the hungry beast she was, and her guttural grunts were a delight to my ears.

Jaime's small member was nothing compared to mine. If I could be bothered to, I could turn him into a nice, beautiful sissy in only a couple of days. He was looking at me with wicked eyes while scrambling on the bed to reach the spot of pleasure he had lost.

I shoved his head with my hand gently before he could get in the way of me rocking his friend. He escaped my weak grasp by pushing my arm aside and reaching out to kiss me tenderly. I let his tongue dominate my mouth before taking control of things. His eyes, which were shut before then, were now wide open in shock. He just realized that, in no way, I would be in a position of submission.

I grabbed his tiny cock with two fingers and stroked it a couple of times. His rigid member shot a rope of jism over the bed, almost hitting the lower side of my belly. He reached over and started to massage my abs. I let him do that while I encouraged him to continue moving down.

I felt so empowered while his small and feeble hands played with my protruding abs. They felt like the wind going up and over steep mountains. I loved how much they were worshiping me right now. The look on their faces suggested they knew I was on top!

I grabbed Jill by her waist, sat on the bed, and slowly put her beside me. Then, I lunged on top of her and started to kiss her smooth lips for what felt like hours. Jaime was feeling a bit lonely, so he got under me to wrap his lips around my glans. Once again, I realized that my cock's thickness was too much for him to handle by himself.

Having seen a large, beautiful chair on the other side of the room, I crawled out of the bed and headed in its direction. Jill and Jaime giggled in delight while they ran after me. Just after I sat on the chair, the two of them kneeled in front of me. I let them reach forward with their tiny little fingers before they enveloped my member with them.

I emitted a long groan of pleasure when I realized that they needed their four hands to fully envelop the whole length of my big man tool. They were looking in awe at my veiny cock before they started to slide the skin up and down. I looked intently at them while their eyes glistened against the blue of the moon outside. Their stares were full of lust!

Jaime started to lick my member from the side, sucking and kissing at the same time while he moved along the full length of my man tool up until the glans. Meanwhile, Jill had her lips all over there, gobbling and making a mess of it as she pleasured me. I placed my hands on their heads to encourage them, which only served to increase their appetite even more.

After all that time playing with them, I was finally close to blowing my load all over them. The two took a couple of steps backward with their knees to prepare for the inevitable. I got back up on my feet and aimed my cock at them.

With all their hunger and appetite growing to stratospheric levels, the two of them opened their mouths and closed their eyes as signs of respect for my throbbing member. I had to hold it tight in my hand to properly aim at their faces.

Jill's and Jaime's faces were painted in white as I blew all my load at them. They were giggling in pleasure as they succumbed to their dirtiest desires. I moaned in pleasure with each rope I jetted toward their long-lost innocence.

When I was done, I plopped into the chair. I could barely keep my eyes open after experiencing so much pleasure and delight. Jill and Jaime still looked as if they had a lot of energy available when they stood back up. I thought they were coming for round two, which I was about to refuse, but then they stepped toward the large, vertical windows of the room.

"What's going on?" I asked with an anemic voice tone. They turned around to look at me, but their faces looked dramatically changed. They were completely distorted now as if the devil himself had come to take control of them.

The air in the bedroom instantly became colder. It felt denser too, which made me have difficulty breathing. I grabbed my neck in a pointless attempt to fill my lungs faster. A dark shadow now covered the faces of the ones who looked so innocent before.

Out of nowhere, snow and ice materialized to cover the ground and walls. I tried to flee from the room, but fell on my ass. Jill and Jaime shouted wicked chuckles while their eyes stared at me.

"Do you know who's about to come, Lucas?" Jill asked, her face still leaning down and her eyes staring at me.

"No", I meekly responded. She laughed maniacally after that

word came out of my mouth.

Before I could even try to get up again, the curtains closed by themselves, covering the bedroom in darkness. I felt the surge of air around me before I completely lost consciousness.

# CHAPTER 4

My eyes slowly opened and met the dimmed moonlight. I turned my head to the side to find out that I was still in the same bedroom as before. The whole environment was completely silent; only the crickets were chirping outside.

"What's going on?" I asked myself, each word coming out as slow as a snail. The air and the whole atmosphere were cold. The ground and walls were still covered with ice and snow.

Something was holding me pinned against the walls. When I looked to find out what it was, I noticed ice covering my hands, keeping me above the floor. Glancing down, I found the same ice keeping my legs immobilized.

My whole body was shivering with how cold the atmosphere was. I squinted my eyes to see if I could find Jill and Jaime in the bedroom, but they were nowhere to be found. Even their clothes, which they took off as we had sex, were gone.

The door, out of the blue, crept open. There was no bright light of hope coming out of it when I noticed none other than Diego stepping in.

"Lucas!" He shouted while running toward me with his arms spread out wide. I tried opening my mouth to ask him to run away from the mansion as fast as he could, but I had no energy for that.

"Diego...", I mumbled, each syllable feeling too hard to pronounce. The chubby young man grabbed a piece of wood from the floor and started to try breaking me free from the ice pins. It didn't work. The ice was much harder and denser than what one could find in a fridge.

"I'm gonna get us out of here!" he promised, each word coming out energized. He almost managed to make me feel some hope, but then I spotted something happening on the other side of the bedroom that quickly made me realize we were screwed.

A thick and dense fog was starting to become denser and collapse around the figure of a person. It was male, tall and he looked strong. Little by little, the muscles and other body parts materialized in front of me.

Having realized I wasn't looking at him, Diego turned on his heels to find the same creature that had just appeared out of a thick and black smoke cloud. He started to try saying something, but his whole body, out of fear, was giving up on him. The creature lifted his arm, pinning my friend against the wall.

He screamed and yelled obscenities. The creature ignored the high-pitched noises as he strode toward us. Ice materialized out of thin air to pin Diego against the wall beside me.

Then, the man-creature disappeared out of the blue and rematerialized in front of Diego. His pants were lowered by the creature, and now he was playing with my friend's tiny cock! The thing that most surprised me wasn't the creature or the condition of the place we were in, but that Diego was an uncut guy!

Diego could barely contain himself as the creature sucked his man tool. I could see its nose rubbing and pushing against the thick pubic hair of my friend. Diego had closed his eyes, opened his mouth wide, and was moaning, his groans unhinged. The creature was giving him immense pleasure.

Minutes later, as if Diego hadn't had sex in a very long time, he blew his load inside the foul mouth of the creature. It opened a nice, sickening smile after he swallowed all the juice from my friend. Diego's head now hung motionless on his neck as the creature stepped toward me. I was still naked, and my cock was already hard as a rock. Having seen what it did to Diego made me scared about what was about to happen to me.

The creature stopped in front of me and eyed me up from

bottom to top. Its blue, cold eyes seemed to penetrate my soul, arousing me to levels beyond what I thought possible.

It cupped my balls and started to play with them. Its fingers were sliding up and down on my testicles, which were pulsating with pleasure. I felt I had a lot of juice in me, even after blowing a lot of it over the faces of Jill and Jaime.

Just when I remembered the sickening faces of the ones who lied to me, they showed up on the other side of the room. Their cold eyes formed a mean glare. I couldn't help but stare back, unable to look elsewhere. They had wicked smiles across their faces, and the lightning and shadow combination served to accentuate their overall grotesque image.

The creature squeezed my balls hard, taking me away from the infinite stare of Jill and Jaime. My cock was hard, oozing pre-cum, and ready to be serviced for the second time in a row. The creature opened a vile smile that sent shivers down my spine. It slowly wrapped its cold, rugged lips around my big man tool. He emitted a muffled moan of pleasure when he was about halfway down the length of my member.

"Stop..." I tried to protest, unable to even move my lips properly. I couldn't help but feel immense amounts of pleasure coming from my cock. It was coming in waves and penetrating the barriers of each of my cells. It was like my head was about to explode when I closed my eyes and the world disappeared around me.

The creature was now deep-throating me, taking every inch I had, and even more when he pushed against my black pubic hair. My whole body was trembling with desire, lust, and pleasure. I wanted much more than that! The creature, by himself, wasn't enough to satisfy me!

Jill and Jaime seemed to have read my mind when I heard their soft footsteps approaching me. Both reached up with their hands to cup my loose testicles. They were playing and fumbling with my rugged ball sack while the man-creature gave me the head of my life.

I felt my cock throbbing once again. My member stiffened

seconds before shooting another generous load, this time all inside the hot interior of its mouth. I looked down to find the creature with its eyes closed, completely oblivious to Jaime and Jill worshiping my scrotum.

More and more of my cum painted his mouth. I could barely control my member as it clashed against his soft lips.

Before long, I was all empty. My ballsack shrank to its normal size, and my cock was starting to soften. The creature opened its ice-cold eyes before showing me another diabolical smile.

Then, the world turned black again when the curtains closed.

# EPILOGUE

I slowly opened my eyes to find myself in front of the mansion. The door to the living room was shut tight. Beside me, lying on the grass, was Diego. His face was buried in the dirt, and saliva was coming out of his mouth.

I slapped his face a couple of times until his eyes crept open. "C'mon, Diego. Wake up. We have to get out here."

"What in the world just happened here…?"

"I don't know", I replied, "But I don't want to come back here."

Maybe it didn't happen at all, since we were both in front of the mansion and the front door looked as if it hadn't been opened in a long time. What was clear, though, was the fact that my cock felt used, taken advantage of, and demoralized.

"Fine. Let's go, then", Diego said while getting up. He offered me his hand, which I gladly took. I looked behind, checking every window to find a clue. None came, and thus I followed Diego to the parking lot.

When we got there, we entered the car and I turned on the engine. The sound of it roaring against the metal chassis was like music to my ears. I closed my eyes shut before pressing my foot on the pedal.

When we got to the main road, Diego grabbed a flier he had in his pocket from the festival.

"Strange…" He started to murmur, "I don't remember getting this from there at all."

"Must've been all the drinks, mate."

"Yeah", he turned the flier around to read the back cover, "There's more here about that mansion."

"Really? And what does it say?"

"Something about a man-creature from the mansion coming back to haunt people every year. Do you think... that this is related to what happened to us?"

Shivers ran down my spine. I immediately looked away from the flier. My hands tightly gripped the steering wheel when I replied with a debile voice, "Hopefully not."

The End

The next page has a steamy sneak peek for the first story of the series. Check it out! Lastly, leave a review if you liked this story. Your feedback helps me improve!

# TEASER: TAKING THEM HARD

Steamy MMF Ménage

*Three Together Is Better - 1*

I just finished landing at the airport. My next objective was to get to the gate where my plane would soon be at. I took my passport and ticket and checked them out, admiring them.

The destination was Raleigh, North Carolina. The airport I was getting out from was in Buenos Aires. I opened my bag and checked out other documents. Some of them were from the college I studied in Argentina, and the rest were from North Carolina State University.

Thanks to a stroke of luck, I secured an internship to study there for one semester. A host there was also kind enough to let me live in his house. I'd never lived in another place before, let alone the house of a total stranger in a different country, so I was nervous.

I tucked all the papers alongside my passport and Visa back into the bag and headed out to explore the airport. It was buzzing with passengers and planes coming and departing all the time.

Chatter was as loud as the sound of the engines.

After some walking, I found myself a bit bored. I was sitting on a chair on the other side of the airport when I thought 'why not?' And grabbed my bag to head to the restrooms.

When I entered the restroom for men, I noticed the very clear and evident smell of piss and shit. No matter, I still had enough time and was bored enough to ignore the unpleasant smell. I opened a stall and entered it without being noticed by the guys in there.

I opened my bag and grabbed my foot-long, realistic dildo. I'd bought it over the internet a couple of months ago and, ever since then, it'd become an important part of my life. I couldn't have a boyfriend since I lived in a conservative family and neighborhood. The twelve inches in length monster was everything I had for the lonely nights.

It had all the bells and whistles someone like me could ask for. Playing with it long enough, it would blow a substance made of milk and honey that tasted and felt just like a man's cum. The dildo was expensive since it was state-of-the-art technology, but definitely worth the money I spent.

I put the dildo on the toilet lid and slowly took off my pants and underwear. Then, while supporting my weight against the walls of the stall, I guided my tight asshole into the fake cockhead. I knew it wasn't going to be easy without some lube, but I didn't want to get myself all wet and oily before my flight.

First, I felt the tip of the cockhead trying to get in. It was fake and felt like silicone and plastic, but it was still very much enjoyable. I had to refrain from moaning when the first inch slid inside. It was rough, but waves of pleasure still intoxicated every cell in my body.

I pushed down farther and felt another inch coming in. More and more jolts of pleasure invaded my immature body.

My hole was shut tight around the plastic member. Once I had about half of it inside me, I started to slide up and down along its length. Powerful. Poised. Thick. That dildo was like magic.

I took more precautions when I started to slide more of the

dildo inside of me. I felt it trembling and getting agitated when I had more than half of it inside of me. Eight bloody inches were already occupying my rectum. Some people would think that it wasn't much, but for me, it was a monstrous length

I kept on pushing more of it inside until I felt it hitting my prostate. My body was trembling and shaking in pleasure. My cockette, much smaller when compared to the monster dildo, was hard and leaking pre-cum like a waterfall. *Shit, I'm gonna have to clean up the puddle on the floor later.*

My nipples, which were small and added to my overall skinny figure, were rock-hard. My body hair was erect when shivers ran down my spine. My ass continued moving up and down, and I now felt little resistance...

# OTHER BICURIOUS SERIES AND MORE

SERIES - BICURIOUS GUYS

Love in the dorm, professors crossing lines, jocks swinging the other way, and more. This series is all about college steam.

1. Caught Looking by the Quarterback
2. Caught Looking by the Basketeer
3. Caught Looking by the Dropout
4. Caught Looking by the Jock
5. Caught Looking by the Roommate

SERIES - GAY FOR BLUE COLLARS

They are massive, thick, and their hands are extra calloused. These blue collars know no boundaries.

1. Given to the Cop
2. Given to the Miner
3. Given to the Plumber
4. Given to the Firefighter
5. Given to the Mechanic

# ABOUT THE AUTHOR

Steamy MM stories, baby! Michael Levi can't go a day without sitting down and putting into words all the dirty scenes that sprout in his mind. His collection is diverse, but it's gay love only. And if you are looking for something free, check his mailing list. Warning: it can be extra spicy.

When Michael Levi isn't writing, he's chilling out by the lake close to his house. Nothing better than kicking back with a martini in his hand as he daydreams his next explicit scenes.